GETTING THE BRUSH OFF

Mere Joyce

ORCA BOOK PUBLISHERS

Library and Archives Canada Cataloguing in Publication

Joyce, Mere, 1988–, author
Getting the brush off / Mere Joyce.
(Orca limelights)

Issued in print and electronic formats.
ISBN 978-1-4598-1358-8 (softcover).—ISBN 978-1-4598-1359-5(pdf).—
ISBN 978-1-4598-1360-1 (epub)

I. Title. II. Series: Orca limelights
PS8619.O975G648 2017   jc813'.6   c2017-900870-6
c2017-900871-4

First published in the United States, 2017
Library of Congress Control Number: 2017933022

Summary: In this high-interest novel for teen readers, Sydney hopes
to win a painting competition to pay for art camp.

*Orca Book Publishers is dedicated to preserving the environment and has printed
this book on Forest Stewardship Council® certified paper.*

Orca Book Publishers gratefully acknowledges the support for
its publishing programs provided by the following agencies:
the Government of Canada through the Canada Book Fund and the Canada
Council for the Arts, and the Province of British Columbia through the
BC Arts Council and the Book Publishing Tax Credit.

Edited by Tanya Trafford
Cover photography by iStock.com

ORCA BOOK PUBLISHERS
www.orcabook.com

Printed and bound in Canada.

20 19 18 17 • 4 3 2 1

*To Finn, for fueling my creativity
and always making me smile.*

One

I know what the people passing by on the boardwalk are thinking.

They're thinking I'm strange. They're thinking I'm wild. They're thinking, *What on earth is she doing?*

They're too busy thinking to actually watch me create.

I stand in a ballet fourth position as I wait for the three beats of silence to tick by before the rapid drumbeat of Wayward Tides, my favorite Maritime punk band, pounds through the salty air of the Halifax Harbour. I drop my arms and spin around in time with the beat, grabbing a brush while I'm still mid-motion.

The people behind me notice the mass of snow-cone-blue hair piled in a messy bun on the top of my head. They notice the small gauges in my ears, and the silver ring in the right corner of my bottom lip. They even notice the ripped skinny jeans and the paint-covered Blondie T-shirt.

But they don't notice how my paintbrush dives into my palette, or how the paint flies through the air as I swoop back to face my easel. They don't notice how the brush slams onto the canvas, making dot after dot of color before I twist the whole canvas sideways and grab a different brush to work with a different shade of paint.

They notice the artist, but they don't notice the art.

Which is exactly how I like it.

I bob my head as I wipe gray paint on the black bandanna wrapped around my wrist. I dip the brush into yellow paint instead and add it to the gray.

"What's going on?" someone whispers from behind me.

"Just watch," someone else replies. I can almost hear the anticipation in their voices, and I love it. I love this.

I lift up onto my toes and do a single pirouette. I peek at my growing audience as I load
my brush and swipe it in a wide arc across the
canvas. The group of onlookers started as only
a couple of young girls, but in the space of two
minutes it's grown to a dozen or more curious
bystanders. Perfect. More people means more
tips. Plus, it gives me a better chance of selling
the finished painting afterward.

I rock my shoulders in time with the music
and raise one leg high in the air in an arabesque
stretch. I grip my extended ankle with my left
hand and bend at the waist—penché!—coming
in close to add fine black dots to the picture I'm
creating. I know what I want this painting to
look like. I knew the moment I started painting
it. It's coming together fast. People don't hang
around on the boardwalk, watching someone
paint, for long. So I've learned how to make an
entire painting in the space of a single song. Now
this one is almost ready. Almost, but not quite.
I haven't completed the show yet.

I place a last tiny dot on the canvas, and then
I throw my paintbrush to the ground as if I'm
furious with it. I flex my fingers, raise them above

3

my head and wiggle them in the air so I know the people watching me can see. Then I bring them down to the small table set up next to my easel, where I keep my supply of paints. I waste no time dipping my fingertips into several different blobs of bluish color, the paint warmed from the midsummer Halifax sun.

This is my favorite part.

I lift my fingers, paint dripping off my nails. I twirl around in a flurried double turn before I push my hands onto the picture, smearing the paint until I've got the colors just right.

A couple of people applaud my dance, and one person laughs when I start using my fingers on the canvas. But their curiosity soon makes them quiet again. The boardwalk around us is busy, but I don't hear the bustle over the beat of my music. I slide my fingers from the center of the painting outward to the edge and then wipe my hands on my shirt. I step back from the painting, taking a few seconds to consider the work as I lip-synch along to the music and play some beats on a set of air drums. Then I prance forward, snatch up a final brush and attack the canvas with short strokes of white paint.

When I'm done, I crouch into a low squat before I pop up into the air, throwing my arms and legs out like a starfish. On my way back down I grab the painting off its easel. I slide into a side split—no easy task in my tight jeans—and place the canvas on the ground before me. I dig my red lipstick out of my pocket, coat my lips and lean my face right down to the bottom edge of the canvas. I kiss the still-wet paint, planting a rim of sticky lipstick in the corner.

Signed with a kiss. Now the painting's done.

I draw my legs in and pull myself up just as the song ends. I wipe paint and lipstick from my mouth and give the crowd a grin. I place the work back on the easel so everyone can see the finished product.

It takes several seconds before the clapping begins. It always does. The people around me don't know what to expect from my performance, but the pretty painting of what they can now see is the Halifax Harbour, with its glistening water, docked tall ships and glowing sunset, still manages to surprise them.

"It's lovely," a woman says, and soon the others agree. Their hands come together to applaud my performance or reach into their pockets for some spare change.

Yes!

I smile modestly, like I've created this painting just for the fun of it and didn't even know anyone was watching.

I just manage to graciously accept my first coins, jangling into the can beneath the hand-painted sign reading *Art by hArt*, when I look up to see the blue suits of two police officers breaking through the crowd.

"Miss Sydney Hart?" one of them asks.

"Yeah, that's me," I reply, giving the pair my sweetest smile.

The first officer glances at my painting, then fixes me with a steady look. "There have been some complaints."

Oh, great.

So much for my tips.

Two

"All right, everyone, if you could just step aside..." The two officers, a doughy young man with kind eyes and a stern woman with graying hair, push their way toward me. It's like I can see all the money I was about to make dropping back into the pockets and purses of each onlooker. I try not to let my face crumple in disappointment as I watch my admirers slink uncomfortably away from the scene.

"Complaints?" I ask, looking at the man who first spoke to me. I'm not doing anything wrong. I'm allowed to busk here on the boardwalk. I'm away from all storefronts, and I'm far enough off the main walkway that I'm not blocking pedestrian traffic.

The man sighs, almost sympathetically. "We've had a complaint about the noise level."

I nearly groan out loud. I dealt with this complaint before, from a souvenir shop with a grumpy owner who kept calling the authorities. But I found a new place to perform, at the other end of the boardwalk. I thought I was safe.

"I'm sorry," I say, doing my best to sound genuinely sad and not just super annoyed. "I'll lower the volume."

The female officer shakes her head and looks at me like she doesn't believe a word I'm saying.

"Miss Hart," she begins, "this is the third complaint we've received this month. I'm afraid you'll have to leave the waterfront area."

"Leave?" It's only two in the afternoon. I had intended to do at least three more performances before the day was out.

The woman nods. "Please pack up your things and go."

"But...but..."

"If you leave now, we'll let you off with another warning," the male officer says. "If you resist, we'll have to issue a fine."

"No, no, I'll go." I turn away from the officers and slump my shoulders, watching the remaining crowd dwindle away. I can't believe I'm losing out on all these tips because of a stupid noise complaint. But I can't stay and argue about it. I'm trying to raise money with my painting, not lose it on a noise violation.

I walk back to my easel and start cleaning up. I wipe the brushes on the bandanna around my wrist, and seal my tubes of paint. Then I drop my painting to the ground so I can collapse the easel and stuff my paints and my speakers into my Gonzo backpack.

When all the supplies are packed, I load the easel and table under one arm, grab the painting with my free hand and stand up. When I do, I come face-to-face with a boy. He's got short brown hair and a tacky string of seashells around his neck.

"Nice painting," he says, and I shrug my shoulders, thrusting the canvas out toward him.

"Want it?" I ask, no longer caring about making a sale. The officers are standing nearby, waiting for me to get going. I take a couple of steps, and the boy rushes to catch up.

"You're just giving it to me?" he asks, surprised. He takes the painting and gives it a long appraisal. "Don't you want to sell it?"

I glance at my work and shrug again before swinging my bag around and unzipping the pouch in Gonzo's mouth. I dig out my phone and send a text to my best friend, Lish.

Done. Meet me @ Historic Properties.

I hit *Send* and then look back up at the boy.

"I won't get anything for it now. I have to sell it as soon as it's painted, or no one will buy it. I've got tons of unsold paintings at home," I explain. "Besides, it's not my best work. The ships are supposed to look like they're bobbing in the water, not just sitting on top of it. I sometimes have trouble getting that effect right."

The boy studies the picture, then smiles. "Well, I like it. It's like something by Monet."

I laugh. "Hardly. It's impressionist style, but it's about a million times less impressive than anything Monet ever painted."

"I still like it. I'll give you something for it," he says, stopping to rest the painting against his leg while he gets out his wallet. He pulls free a twenty-dollar bill. "Here."

I consider refusing the money, but then remember my lost sale.

"Thanks," I say, pocketing the bill and smirking when he continues to follow me.

"You're really good," he says, holding the painting proudly out before him.

"Thanks," I say again, even though I'm not sure whether he really likes my work or is just humoring me.

He seems to notice my skeptical expression.

"No, I mean it," he declares. "You've got talent. In fact..." He holds the picture in one hand and tugs a folded pamphlet from the front pocket of his jeans with the other. "I think you might be interested in this."

I take the pamphlet cautiously. People hand out weird things on the boardwalk. Once someone shoved a brochure for a cult in my face while I was waiting in line to get an ice-cream cone.

"What is it?" I ask, unfolding the glossy paper. I spot the Burke Arts Academy logo at the top of the page. My stomach drops, and I have to remind myself to breathe.

"It's a speed-painting competition," the boy says, pointing to an ad on the brochure's front page. "I think you should enter. The Burke Academy is a good school. You know it, right?"

"Uh, yeah," I mutter. "I've heard of it." I stare at the brochure, the name of the school sending unpleasant shivers down my spine.

I know the school, all right.

I used to go there, before Mom lost her job and we could no longer afford the tuition. I used to dance there, before I was forced to give up my instruction and any hope of a dancing future. I used to have a best friend there, before she decided she didn't want to hang out with an academy reject.

I used to have an entire life at the Burke Arts Academy. But I never expected to have anything to do with the school ever again.

"Yeah, well..." The boy smiles uncertainly and holds up the painting once more. "You should enter. Think about it, at least. Anyway, I've got to go. Thanks again!"

I don't even notice as the boy walks away. I'm still staring at the brochure.

Three

I read the advertisement at least three times. It's the first brush-off competition the Burke Arts Academy has ever held. It's open to painters across Nova Scotia aged fourteen through seventeen, which puts me right in the middle since I just turned sixteen last month. I've heard of competitions like this before, but I've never been to one. I've never really thought of my performances as speed-painting either. But the winner gets two hundred dollars cash, plus a mystery prize to be revealed at the competition.

The two hundred dollars is enough for me.

"Sydney! Over here!"

I look up from the brochure and scan the boardwalk for the voice calling my name.

Lish is easy to spot in the crowd. For one thing, she's waving her arms above her head, trying to get my attention. For another, she's the only girl in sight with dark skin and candy-floss-pink hair. I grin and rush to meet her, immediately grabbing the massive fountain drink out of her hand and taking a long sip. I didn't even realize I was thirsty, but the soda is cold and wonderfully sweet as it trickles down my throat.

"Why are you finished so soon? I thought you were going to be out all day," Lish says softly.

Lish has the most beautiful voice I've ever heard. Her parents are from St. Lucia, and she was born in England. Her family came to Canada when Lish was ten, but her voice has retained both the English accent of her childhood and the Caribbean influence of her family. She's a brilliant singer too, even if she only ever sings when she's piecing together her latest sewing project. Lish is more interested in fashion than anything else. She loves scouring weekend garage sales to find things she can upcycle into unique accessories. Hence her handmade Miss Piggy backpack that matches the Gonzo pack she made me for my last birthday.

"I was," I say, handing back her drink. "The cops shut me down."

"What? You're kidding, right?" Lish gives me a scolding look, her normally wide eyes narrowed sternly. "This isn't because of your music again, is it?"

"Uh...no?"

"Sydney!" Lish whacks me on the shoulder, and I feign pain, rubbing the spot and pouting my lip.

"I can't paint without my music—you know that," I say defensively.

Lish shakes her head. "Yes, but do you have to play it so loud? I thought you wanted to save up enough money for art camp."

"I do," I mumble, thinking about how, even after today's sale, I'm still a hundred dollars short of the funds needed to join next month's art camp at the Nova Scotia College of Art and Design. I've only got a few weeks left to save up the rest of the money. Not even enough time to find a job flipping burgers.

"Well, you'd better think of something," Lish says. She studies me for a moment before she clicks her tongue and smiles. "Who was that boy

I saw you with?" she asks. I clench the Burke Arts Academy brochure in my fist as she says it. She notices the paper crumpling up. She reaches for my fist, pries my fingers open and grabs the brochure.

"He was just telling me about some stupid art competition," I say as casually as I can. "Nothing important."

"Burke Arts Academy…isn't that where you used to go to school?" Lish says, glancing up at me, one eyebrow quirked so high it disappears under her pink bangs.

"Yeah, it is," I mumble, looking down at the brochure.

"Is this the competition? The Brush Off?"

"I guess so. I didn't really look at it," I lie.

"Timed, live speed-painting competition for teens fourteen through seventeen? Sydney, this is perfect for you!" Lish gives me an excited look, and I grab the paper back, stuffing it into my pocket next to the twenty bucks from the mysterious boy.

"No, it's not. It's being hosted by the Burke Academy," I say. Lish doesn't respond, and I give her a pointed look. "Which means it takes place at the academy. Lish, I can't go back there! They kicked me out, remember? The day I left that world was the most humiliating day of my life. I don't intend to revisit the memories anytime soon."

Lish takes a long, slow sip of her drink and then crosses her arms over her chest. "You want to go to this art camp, don't you?" she asks, and I let out a tired breath, wondering again how I'll make up the rest of my needed funds.

"Yeah, of course I do," I say.

"Well?" Lish waits for me to say something else. I stare at her blankly until she rolls her eyes and points at my pocket. "Did you even read the whole ad? Goodness, girl, what would you do without me?" She leans forward and pulls out the tattered brochure again. "Look here. See what it says? Cash prize."

"Yeah, I know. I did see it," I say, but I study the advertisement again anyway.

The words on the cream-colored page are tempting. A cash prize would be wonderful. And two hundred dollars would be more than enough to get me to art camp.

But is the money for camp worth revisiting the school I used to call my home? Is it worth revisiting the life I used to have?

Four

When I get home, I go straight to my room. My fluffy, orange cat, Ember, is sprawled across the center of my bed. Flopping onto the bed beside him, I run my fingers through his thick fur.

"Hey, Ember," I mutter, nuzzling my face against his as he purrs his consent.

I pet Ember for several minutes before I roll onto my back and tug the brochure from my pocket again. I reread the ad on the front for about the fifth time, and then I open it up to look at the rest of the pages. There are pictures of girls in ballet shoes, boys dancing in tuxedos, violin players, art instructors, students laughing under the massive oak tree in the school's inner courtyard. I look at the happy group of models and notice a familiar face among them.

Miranda Wakefield. My former best friend.

It's not surprising she's in these pictures. Mrs. Wakefield is the head of practically every committee in the local arts community, and Miranda makes a perfect choice for a model. She's pretty, but not too glamorous. She looks approachable, like she's sweet and sincere.

I snort and drop the pamphlet onto my bed.

Miranda Wakefield seems sweet enough upon first glance. But I remember all too clearly how fast she turned cold and nasty once I was no longer a part of the academy.

A knock at my door makes me jump.

"Who is it?" I ask, as if I don't already know. Only one person ever bothers to knock around here.

"It's me!" a little voice shouts, and I climb off the bed. I walk to the door and open it to see my six-year-old half brother, Ethan, rocking back and forth on his heels. "Mom wants to know if you're going to be home for dinner."

I lean against the doorframe and weigh my options. If I stay at home, I'll get good food for free, but I'll have to deal with Mom's looks of disdain regarding my hair and, since more recently, my lip ring.

My relationship with my mother has always been strained. It was bearable when I attended Burke full time and she could only scold me about my posture or my fondness for chocolate on weekend visits. But since I left the academy two years ago, she's been desperate to keep me in perfect shape in case she ever lands a new job making enough money to re-enroll me. At first I kept up appearances too. But eventually I realized I wasn't ever getting my old life back. So I created a new one, which my mother hates.

"Yeah, I guess I'll stick around," I tell Ethan with a sigh. I'd love to avoid Mom, especially after this afternoon's discovery of the brush-off competition. But I'm starving, and I don't want to waste money buying myself food.

Ethan looks up at me with his big brown eyes. Mostly Ethan looks like his father, Charlie, but we both share our mother's eyes.

"Your hair is really blue today," he says with a smile, and I smirk, pulling out my ponytail and letting the strands fall down to the middle of my back.

"I got it redone yesterday. You like?"

"I like." Ethan nods. At least someone in this family does. Considering it's the one thing I'm willing to spend my savings on, it's nice to see it appreciated by someone other than Lish.

"I'm glad," I say, and Ethan ducks in to give my legs a quick hug.

"I'll tell Mom you're staying," he says. He releases his grip and bounds away down the hall.

I shake my head in amusement as I close the door and pull my hair back into a long ponytail. Ethan likes having me around, but our mom and his dad were both less stressed when I lived at the academy several miles away.

The problem is, they think I'm rebelling. They're always telling me to grow up and be more responsible. But I'm not irresponsible, and I'm not immature.

I'm just different.

When I started ninth grade at my new school two years ago, I needed an elective, but most of the classes were already full. So they stuck me in art. For the first month I couldn't stand it. Then I discovered I actually loved it. Painting taught me how to channel my emotions through mood and color. I felt very blue in those days. I used a lot of blues in my paintings because I was always sad. And then one day I realized I wasn't sad anymore, but I still liked painting with blue. I learned to love the color, not for its sadness, but for its brightness and its beauty.

I walk back to my bed and look at the Burke Academy brochure again. The Brush Off is next weekend. And the deadline for entering is tomorrow. Whoever the boy at the boardwalk was, he sure had great timing.

I stare at the picture of the students sitting under the oak tree. I remember the days when I would have fit in perfectly with those models. When my hair was a deep brown and conditioned constantly to keep it sleek and manageable. When my skin was pale and delicate instead of tanned and pierced. When I kept rigid control of my diet. Now I'm fifteen pounds heavier—but fifteen pounds more comfortable.

Being at the academy was great, and I still miss it. But despite my mother's aggravation,

I like where I am now too. If I were to go back to Burke today, I'd probably realize I'd never want to return there as a student anyway.

At least, it's what I tell myself. It's how I convince myself to pick up my phone and send another text off to Lish.

I'm doing it. I'm entering the brush off.

Five

One week later, I return to the school I never thought I'd set foot in again.

"Wow, this is where you went? It's like a museum in here." Lish walks in a slow circle around the Burke Academy's main foyer. Her flip-flops smack against the white-gray marble floor with each step. The resulting sound gives me goose bumps. I remember tap-dancing in this hall between classes, practicing for days just to try and pass Madame Aubin's rigorous exams.

"Come on," I say. I'm relieved it's still summer and the students of the academy are not around. I'm not sure I could take seeing the halls crammed full of leg warmers, leotards, instrument cases or even splattered and stained painting smocks.

I grab Lish by the arm and drag her across the foyer to the sweeping staircase leading up to the second-floor art studio.

"Seriously though," Lish says, her eyes wandering over every inch of the dark wood-paneled walls. "This is like something out of a movie. No wonder you miss it."

"I don't miss it because the building's nice," I say, although being here makes me realize I do miss the school's century-old hallways and classrooms. Living at the academy suited me. I remember winter nights by the fire in our dorm's common room. I remember ghost stories about the lonely ballerinas and orphaned servant boys who supposedly haunt the place. And I remember dance, all kinds of dance. In the rainy spring or the cool autumn. In the mornings before sunrise or at dusk and until well past midnight.

I'm sad I don't remember painting. I never discovered my love for the canvas until after I'd left this world behind.

"Yeah, but the building is gorgeous," Lish says, and I can't disagree. So I just give her arm another tug and pull her down the second-floor corridor to the art studio.

It's packed inside. I was expecting to see my opponents, the judges and some friends and family. But I didn't plan on opening the studio's doors to find a mass of people huddled by the registration desk or filling the chairs set up in a wide circle and along the large studio's walls. There must be fifty or more audience members alone.

Fifty people watching me paint!

I'm not shy. I'm used to painting in front of people, and dancing in front of people too. But as I make my way inside the room, I'm very aware of the stares directed at me and Lish. Specifically, at our clothes and our hair.

This competition is open to the public, and I thought I'd see artists of every type getting ready to show off their talents. But either the pool of willing participants is small, or, more likely, this competition hasn't been well advertised. At least, not outside the academy's inner circles.

The painters I see around me look like they've just stepped out of the Burke Arts Academy brochure. There are girls and guys both, most of them with perfect posture and new outfits void of specks or creases. No one else has blue hair, which is not surprising. But I don't see a single ragged shirt, tattoo, shaved head or even any piercings other than the odd sparkle from a pair of diamond earrings.

I guess artists don't have to look outlandish. But I hadn't planned on being the only person in the entire competition with a unique sense of style. Normally I'd count this as an advantage. But the laughing sneers I get as I gaze around the room tell me my look isn't a point in my favor today.

Once I would have slipped into this room completely unnoticed, just another Burke Academy girl without a single strand of hair out of place. Right now I kind of wish I looked like my former self again.

"Hey, isn't that the guy you were with at the boardwalk?" Lish points through the crowd, finding the one pair of friendly eyes looking our way. The boy who gave me the brochure last weekend waves and pushes his way passed a group of chatting painters.

"You came," he says as a greeting.

"Yeah, and I'm wondering if I should have. This is open to everyone, right? I didn't actually ask when I called to sign up."

He laughs. "Yeah, it is, although you wouldn't know it." He glances around the room and then turns to grin at Lish. "Are you entering too?" he asks.

Lish lets out a laugh of her own. "No way," she says. "I can't paint. Besides, this place isn't for me."

"I highly doubt it's for either of you," a cold voice says from behind us.

My shoulders tense.

I recognize the sharp cut of the words and the smooth way they slip from the lips of the girl who spoke them.

I turn around slowly and find myself face-to-face with Miranda.

My former best friend stares at me with slender eyebrows arched in haughty disapproval. I haven't seen Miranda for nearly two years, since shortly after I left the academy. At that time, we were equal in the way we carried ourselves, in the precise way we kept ourselves composed. Now I probably look like a wild animal compared to her neatly combed blond hair and perfectly applied makeup.

I meet Miranda's gaze and wait for a reaction I don't get. She stares at me as if she's never seen me before.

I open my mouth to see if I can jog her memory with the sound of my voice. But before I can speak, a slim, gray-haired older woman—Ms. Camford, the academy's headmistress—speaks instead.

"Ladies and gentlemen," she begins in a firm, commanding tone, "if you haven't registered, please do so now, and set up your easel immediately. The competition will begin shortly."

"Go on," Lish whispers, nudging my side and ignoring Miranda altogether. "Get set up. I'll be over there." She jerks a thumb toward a row of chairs near the back of the room. Then she looks at the boy standing before us. "See you later, boy," she smiles.

He grins, giving her a nod. "It's Jorge," he says. He gives me a last smiling glance as well, and then he heads to one of the easels already set up. I didn't know he was competing. Why would he encourage me to join the brush off, if he is competing too?

Unless, of course, he expects me to fail. My stomach clenches, and I let out a long, slow breath as I move toward the registration table to sign in.

I take a single step forward before Miranda pushes past me, scowling as she glides by on the way to her easel.

So she's competing as well.

Great.

I'm starting to think I may have made a big mistake.

Six

Ms. Camford addresses the painters, each one standing by an easel set up in a circle around the center of the room. "There will be three rounds of painting," the headmistress explains. "Two today and one tomorrow. Our first round is comprised of twenty-seven painters. This will be narrowed to fifteen for this afternoon's second round, and five competitors will compete in our auditorium in the final round tomorrow." She stands in the middle of us all, glancing at each of us as she talks. When she looks at me, I lower my eyes. Ms. Camford was the one who told me and my mother I could no longer attend the academy. I don't want to draw her attention.

I don't want to draw *anyone*'s attention. At this moment I'm wishing I had never even thought about entering this competition. I could have raised the money for my camp somewhere else. I could have saved myself the humiliation of being in a place where I'm not allowed to belong.

"Each round will have a theme," Ms. Camford continues. She walks in a lazy circle around the room, her high heels tapping sternly against the art studio's polished-wood floor. "Painters can interpret the theme as they wish. For this first round, there will be a time limit of fifteen minutes. Afterward there will be a short recess while our judging panel determines which paintings will advance to the next round."

I glance uneasily around the room. Miranda holds her head up high, her hands behind her back and a gentle smile on her lips. Jorge stands two easels away from her, his stance more relaxed. I try not to think of his reasons for inviting me to join this competition. I try not to think of the way Miranda walked past me without even knowing who I was.

"The winner will receive a cash prize of two hundred dollars," Ms. Camford says, coming to a standstill in the center of the circle. Her back is to me, and I'm grateful for it. "But I am happy to announce an additional incentive for the young painters among us this morning. Our judges will be on the lookout for technique, interpretation of theme, and personality. The winning artist will receive not only the two hundred dollars but also the mystery prize."

I forgot all about the mystery prize. Probably because I don't care. I came for the cash, and now I'm not sure even the money was worth the trip.

"The mystery prize for this weekend's brush-off winner is a Burke Arts Academy scholarship for full tuition and board," Ms. Camford says.

My body goes rigid. My hands start to tremble. *What did she just say?*

"This scholarship, the first of its kind, has been graciously donated by the Galbraith family of Halifax," the headmistress explains. "As the family wished the scholarship to be given to a deserving young artist, we have decided to offer it as the grand prize for this competition."

Excited chatter breaks out throughout the room. The academy has never offered a scholarship before, let alone one for full tuition plus living expenses. Even for the kids who already attend the academy, a scholarship would save them money and look great on university applications.

I glance behind me at the audience and try to distinguish who the judges might be. The name Galbraith sounds familiar, but I can't pick out any obvious possibilities from the crowd. They aren't sitting in a row, waiting with pen and paper to mark us with scores out of ten. They're hidden.

But I suppose it doesn't matter who the judges are. It doesn't matter who the Galbraith family is either. If I impress everyone, I'll impress them.

And I have to impress them. Because as soon as Ms. Camford announced the scholarship, I realized how badly I want to win it. I like my life now, but I can't deny how much I miss this school. I belonged here once. Suddenly I have the opportunity to belong here again.

I never took an art class in the three years I attended the Burke Academy. But Miranda did, and I know the school's art instructors are some of the best in the province. I can't pass up the chance to study with them. Attending art camp is nothing compared to the chance of once more being a Burke girl.

"If our painters are ready..." Ms. Camford says, interrupting my thoughts. The room quiets down almost instantly. I take a deep breath and try to ignore the staggering beat of my heart. I glance at the other painters. They all seem completely calm and composed. Am I the only one worried about the next fifteen minutes? I look at their straight backs and their simple, stylish clothes. I cringe at the thought of what the judges must already think of me.

Ms. Camford holds up an old-fashioned ticking stopwatch. "We will now begin the competition," she says.

I drag my eyes back to my easel. I stare at the canvas before me. I get ready to grab a brush.

"The first theme is 'life.' And your fifteen minutes starts now."

Seven

The room fills with the rustle of artists mixing their paints and getting to work. We were allowed to bring our own supplies, and I decided on using watercolor paints today. When I paint outside, I usually use acrylics. They're faster to set up because they don't require any mixing ahead of time. On the boardwalk, a quick setup is a must. But here I had time to fill a bowl of water in the studio sink and mix some colors so they were ready to be used. The shades are laid out on the palette now, and the brushes are lined up beside them, just waiting for me to take hold and get started.

The other painters have already begun. I can hear brushes on canvas. I can smell the paints and the almost caramel-like odor of the floor polish.

I can see a white square before me, ready to be decorated.

I grip a brush and hold it over my selection of colors.

What am I going to paint? How am I going to turn the theme of "life" into a picture worthy of the judges' attention?

My left hand pats the pocket of my jeans, where I've placed my phone and my earbuds. I always listen to music while I paint. It helps me focus. But I can't listen to it now. No one else here has music playing, and they're all doing fine. It wouldn't look good if I stuck my earbuds in and started bobbing my head to the rhythm. They'd think I wasn't taking this seriously.

I dip my brush into black paint and raise it to the canvas. Three minutes have already slipped by, and I haven't even started. Of course, when I paint on the boardwalk, I make my entire creations in the length of a single song. But if I whip up something that quick now, they'll think I couldn't come up with a worthwhile idea.

I don't have an idea. I don't know how to interpret such a vague theme. But I try to appear as though I'm considering the angle at which I want to make my first stroke. Another minute slithers past, and I know I can't hold out any longer. With a trembling hand, I place the brush on the canvas and make a black line down the center of the square.

Wait...did I just start with black? What have I done? Why did I start with black?

Panic sets in. I hurry to come up with an idea not totally unworkable. I force my brain to start thinking.

Black. Black. Isn't black reserved for death?

I study the line and see it's crooked. Wrong color, and the wrong shape. Two mistakes already, and I've only made one stroke. But maybe I can work with crooked. I dip my brush in the black again and add to the line, making it thicker. I splay it out at the bottom of the canvas, giving it roots.

A tree. A dead tree.

Loads of dead trees.

The idea comes, and finally the picture starts to take shape. I flip my brush around so the end of it faces the canvas, and I scratch through the black paint to give the tree a sgraffito effect. Then I whip the bristles across the picture, making the big tree in the middle of the painting as ugly as possible. I paint limp and broken branches, and add a pile of black and dusty gray leaves on the ground by the trunk. Then I add more trees in the background, varying their sizes, drawing some with blurry edges while others are sharper and more distinct.

There's no music playing, but I tap my foot on the floor as if there were. I lift myself up on my toes, desperate to dance as the ideas of the painting flow. I add a quick blue-gray mist to the air around the trees, the watercolors bleeding into the canvas and giving the whole scene a creepy, foggy look.

"Five minutes remaining, painters," Ms. Camford says, and I close my eyes for a moment, imagining how I want the finished painting to appear. I picture it, and I smile, nodding my head to the beat of some unheard song. But when I open my eyes again, I catch the gaze of the painter next to me, an Asian girl with scornful amusement in her eyes.

Embarrassed, I stop moving. I hold my body perfectly still and clear away any hint of a song playing in my head.

I pick up a new brush and mix a bit of dark green and tawny brown. I add it to the canvas, my hand moving awkwardly, my wrist bending at the wrong angle and the paint splotching an inch higher than it should. If I use my fingers, I can fix it. I can draw the paint down in a line and smear it so the mistake looks intentional. But I'm positive no one else is using their fingers here. It seems so childish now, I can't believe I ever thought it was a good idea to use mine.

I take an unused brush and do my best to fix the paint. I brush the splotch down into a too-thick line and then add more color, drawing small leaves off of a single green stalk. When it's done, I add the faintest glimmer of a yellow ray of sun beaming down over the tiny plant.

"One minute," Ms. Camford informs us.

If I were on the boardwalk or in my own room, I'd add a few last-second details to this work. But I don't want to risk messing it up more than I already have. Instead, I focus on signing it. It's a task I usually do with my lipstick. But not today. Today I take a thin brush and dab it with black paint. I hold it near the bottom of the picture and make an uneven attempt at my own name.

S. Hart.

I drop the brush on the little table next to my easel and take a step back. The vision of a dark and dreary forest full of dead trees, with one single green plant rising from the barren land, is okay. But only okay. It's not great. I'm fairly certain it's not quite good enough.

I feel like crying, but I have no time to form any tears before Ms. Camford is walking back into the circle of painters.

"Time's up!" she says with a small smile. I keep my chin raised and try not to let my disappointment show.

Eight

Ms. Camford tells us there will be a twenty-minute break before the results of the first round are announced. We are welcome to stay and look at the other paintings if we wish. Every painter is instructed to turn his or her easel around so the paintings all face the middle of the room for judging. As the easels scrape along the floor, I see picture after impressive picture come into view.

Of all the entries, mine is the darkest. Apparently, no one else thinks using a lot of black is appropriate when creating a scene based on life.

"Ooh, moody! I like it." Lish approaches my painting and gives me an approving nod.

"It's horrible," I say glumly, but Lish waves my concern away.

"It's great," she says. I'd like to believe her, but Lish thinks everything I do is great.

"Well, that's an interesting take on the theme..."

I hear the whispers behind me, but I refuse to look back and acknowledge I've heard them. Instead I rest my forehead on Lish's shoulder and loop my arm around hers.

"Let's go for a walk," I mumble. "I've got twenty minutes left before I find out officially that I didn't make it to the next round. I don't want to spend them staring at my miserable attempt."

"Fine by me. This room is ridiculously hot. They should've capped the number of people who could stay and watch."

I grab my Gonzo backpack and head for the door. On the way out of the room, I pass by Miranda's easel. She's painted an orange-spotted turtle resting next to a clutch of eggs, one small hatchling peeking out from a broken shell. It's not exactly what I would call an inspiring image, but her technique is flawless. Miranda has been a top pupil at Burke—in art, dance and just about every other subject—since the sixth grade, which is the first year students can attend the academy.

We'll both be going into grade eleven in September, but for Miranda, the fall will mark her sixth year as a Burke girl. I wonder what it would be like to have five years of art training like she does.

She's too busy talking with Ms. Camford to notice me slinking past. When I pass by Jorge's easel, though, he catches my eye immediately. He follows Lish and me as we exit the room.

"Nice job," he says, stretching his arms over his head. "Although lacking a bit of your usual finesse."

I roll my eyes, annoyed by his smirk. "Sorry. I didn't humiliate myself for your amusement," I snap.

Jorge's face registers surprise, and he exchanges a look with Lish. "I didn't mean...I just figured you'd be a bit more outgoing," he says, his voice apologetic. "It's still good though. Original."

"Yeah, and *original* means 'bad,'" I grumble.

"Yours was pretty good too, boy," Lish says, ignoring me.

"It's Jorge," Jorge replies, but he smiles as if he's flattered by her attention. "And thanks. I've had the idea for that painting for a while now. But I needed more time to really make it complete." Jorge painted a pastel portrait of a pregnant woman.

A simple concept, but a lovely painting all the same. "I'm not good with speed-painting. I need to take my time to make my projects shine."

"So why are you in the competition?" Lish asks, and Jorge shrugs his shoulders.

"Who wouldn't want to win a full scholarship and get two hundred bucks too?"

"Wait." I stop in the middle of the second-floor corridor and turn to look at Jorge. "You knew about the scholarship?"

"Sure," he says, shoving his hands into the pockets of his freshly pressed trousers. "No one said anything official until today, but there were rumors. Everyone here knew about it. That's why there are so many people in the competition."

"Everyone here. You attend Burke?" I ask. Jorge nods. I eye him suspiciously. I still don't understand why he invited me to join the competition, especially if he knew about the mysterious grand prize.

We fall into silence as we walk. We cover the entire second floor before heading back into the art studio to hear the judges' decision. I mope, feeling sorry for myself. I should have known I couldn't compete in a place like this, looking like I do. Two years ago I would have laughed to see someone like me standing alongside students of the academy.

Someone like me.

I feel sick. I'm supposed to like who I am. I did—until this morning.

When we get back to the art studio, I expect to hear Ms. Camford asking us to gather around as she lists off the names of the semifinalists. Instead, we arrive to discover the entries have already been chosen. The successful easels are marked with a blue ribbon, like the kind handed out at county fairs.

Miranda's turtles have a ribbon. Two easels away, I see Jorge's pregnant lady has one too.

And halfway across the room, dangling beneath my dark and dreary forest, is a blue ribbon of my own.

"See?" Jorge says, pointing to my work. "Originality counts for something."

I run my fingers through my blue hair and study the blue ribbon pinned to my easel. I guess originality does count for something, even in a place like this.

I'm just not sure it counts for enough.

Nine

Somehow I've made it to the second round. I was lucky. But I can't rely on luck to get me through round two. If I want to make it to the final tomorrow, I need a plan.

"Where are you going?" Lish calls after me, rushing to catch up as I hurry from the room and speed toward the staircase.

"To get supplies," I say, taking the steps down two at a time.

"Um, don't you have everything you need already?" Lish asks, confused by my sudden flight. I pause briefly at the bottom of the stairs to wait for her.

"Not painting supplies. I need supplies for me. For my look," I tell her.

Lish eyes me uncertainly. "I have no idea what you're talking about."

I sigh and grab her arm as I start walking again. "I need to win that scholarship, Lish. I have to get back into this school."

"Wait, what about art camp?" Lish asks.

I throw my hands into the air. "Who cares about art camp?"

"Well, up until five minutes ago I thought you did," Lish says flatly.

"Yes, but...I'll still be able to go to camp if I win," I remind her. "And if I get back into Burke, I'll get something better than art camp. I'll get a future. With a school like Burke on my university applications, I'll be able to get into the Nova Scotia College of Art and Design for more than just camp. Or I could go somewhere in Toronto. Or Vancouver. Even outside of Canada, if I wanted! The Burke Academy makes anything possible."

"Okay, fine," Lish says slowly. We're on the street outside the academy. I want to find a clothing shop, preferably one where I can buy an entire outfit for less than a hundred bucks. It's all the money I have on me. Plus, if I only spend a hundred, I'll still have just enough left to pay my camp dues.

If I win the brush off, of course. Which is why I need a new outfit in the first place.

"But I still don't understand why you need supplies," Lish says impatiently.

I look down at my faded jeans and my baggy purple T-shirt with the hole in one side. "If I want to win the scholarship, I have to look like I belong at the school. And right now, I don't. So I'm going to fix what I can before the next round starts." We were given two hours for lunch before the brush off continues this afternoon. Which means I've got about an hour and a half to get everything I need.

"You're going to change your look to impress the judges?" Lish stares at me like I've gone crazy. Maybe I have. But if crazy is what it takes to win back my place at Burke, then so be it.

"Yes," I say firmly, jogging across the street. "Now come on!"

Lish shakes her head, but she follows me anyway.

We find a store with a good discount rack of last season's clothing. Lish helps me pick out an outfit I can afford, digging through the rack for hidden gems. I end up with a pair of black jeans, a cheap pair of black flats and a cream-colored top three sizes too big but which Lish expertly safety-pins so it looks purposefully loose and billowy. I change into my new outfit right in the store.

I don't have time to get my hair done, or else I'd run to a salon and beg them to strip the color. I've never regretted my blue hair until now. It's a disappointing way to feel, after loving the shade for so long. But blue hair is not what the Burke Academy wants. I can't recall anyone in the school even having colored highlights during the years I went there. It's probably in the school handbook or something. *Thou shalt not dye thine hair.*

But I can't change the color now, so I make the best of the situation. In the bathroom of a nearby coffee shop, Lish braids it and then twists the braid up so it hangs close to the nape of my neck. I take the black bandanna from my wrist. I turn it inside out, hiding the paint splotches. I tie it around my head, covering my hair completely.

I study my altered reflection in the bathroom mirror.

"You look very...boring," Lish says. She watches as I carefully pull out the silver ring from my lip, her expression pained. Lish has always wanted a lip ring, but her parents won't allow it. "Very boring," she pouts as I stand up straight, admiring the plain view.

"Perfect," I say, turning one way and then the other. I may not be as proper as Miranda, but with a little polishing, I could fit right in with the academy. It's almost like looking at a mirror to the past. This is me a month or two after being kicked out of Burke. Stressed and a bit sloppy, but almost an ideal student.

It's good enough for such short notice.

Except for one final thing.

I glance down at my Gonzo backpack, my favorite Muppet staring back at me with his blue lidded eyes.

"I can't take him in with me," I say, a pang of discomfort rippling through my stomach. I love my backpack. And I love how Lish made it for me. I look at her now with pleading eyes, and she stares up at the ceiling.

"Can you believe her?" she says to no one in particular. She grabs my pack and hauls it onto her shoulder, Gonzo and Miss Piggy riding side by side.

I give Lish a quick hug, and then I grin.

"Let's get back," I say. The second round is about to begin. And this time, I know exactly what I'm doing.

Ten

We get back with only minutes to spare. When we fly into the art studio, the easels of the painters who didn't make it to the second round have already been removed. The remaining easels have been turned back around and pushed farther apart to give us more space.

"Where did you disappear to? I thought you weren't coming back..." Jorge trails off as he takes in my new look. He looks me up and down, then frowns. "Whoa. What happened to you?"

"She's decided bland is the new fashion statement of the year," Lish says and sighs, and I roll my eyes, moving to my canvas and checking to make sure everything is still set up the way I need it.

"I just want to look professional," I explain. "Do you honestly think I'd stand a chance of winning the scholarship looking like I did this morning?"

"Well, it got you this far, didn't it?" Jorge asks. He sounds annoyed.

"They needed something to entertain the crowd," I mutter. I catch Lish's skeptical glance and give her an exasperated stare in return. "The scholarship won't go to someone with ragged clothes and blue hair," I say.

"Whatever," Lish replies. She turns to Jorge and smiles. "Good luck, boy."

"It's Jorge," Jorge says again. Lish doesn't reply. She turns and walks to a seat behind my easel so she can watch me paint. Jorge follows her with his eyes and then turns and heads over to his own easel. Neither of them wishes me good luck. I don't really care about Jorge's lack of encouragement, but Lish's silence hurts.

"We'll now begin our second round," Ms. Camford says, distracting me. "For this round, painters will have ten minutes. The top five will then move on to the final round tomorrow afternoon."

I glance over to where Jorge and Miranda now stand next to one another. I take a deep, slow breath. This time I know I can compete with them. This time I won't even hesitate. This time I've got the mindset of a true Burke Academy artist.

Ms. Camford pulls out her stopwatch as she speaks. "The theme for this round is 'sight.'"

I focus on the canvas before me. I lift a hand, ready to grab a brush.

"Your time starts now."

I get an idea immediately. A pair of eyes staring out through goggles, with a futuristic landscape reflected in the goggles' lenses. I can envision color, emotion and a wicked design. But I push the idea out of my head and search for another. Funky and fun is not what will get me the scholarship. I need to think of something more traditional, something to showcase my technique instead of my imagination.

I take a brush and mix a light white-gray. I put the brush on the canvas and swoop the bristles in soft curves near the top of the square. Clouds. I paint several clouds, and then I quickly scribble a green forest along the bottom, making the trees tiny and far away, as if the painting is being done from high up in the sky. I add a beach, dot the canvas over and over again with beige and yellow pinpoints of color to make the sand. I add glistening water and use white paint to create sparkles on the surface where the water swells up into gentle waves.

Then I start in on the main feature of the painting. I pull my brush in a zigzag to create the look of feathers at the edges of the canvas. I dapple them with black paint at first, then apply a deep red, using the broken-color technique favored by the Impressionists to give the feathers a sleek, glossy quality.

"Five minutes remaining," Ms. Camford announces.

I finish the outline of two widespread wings. I pause to ensure the feathers are even on both sides of the picture. I add a bit more length to the feathers on the left before I start to shade them with color. Then I get to work crafting a beak peeking out at the uppermost edge of the picture.

"One minute remaining."

I study the painting, then use my last minute to make the whole picture as even as possible. I add a few more trees to the forest and then make a fast flourish with my brush to paint the remaining white space a dull, hazy blue. Last of all, I make a careful signature in the bottom corner. My lips twitch, longing to kiss the painting. I press them together and finish with my brush.

No music. No dance. No fun of any kind. I feel like I've just taken an exam.

"Time's up!"

I step back and view the finished painting. I've successfully captured the illusion of a bird high above the tree line, a lush, grand landscape seen from its soaring perspective. The colors are correct, and the angles are just right. It is, structurally, one of the best paintings I've ever done.

But I'm strangely dissatisfied with it. I keep thinking about the painting I would have done if I'd been on my own or out on a public street. The goggles reflecting the futuristic world. It would have been a totally different piece, but it would have had a lot more personality. And it would have been a lot more fun.

I look down at my feet as Ms. Camford asks us to turn our easels. My black flats are plain and boring, just like my painting. But, just like my painting, I think they're exactly what fits into this competition and this school.

Eleven

Jorge tells me my painting is nice, but his voice is flat when he says it. He didn't finish his picture of an old blind man being guided across a busy intersection by a young child, which is too bad. The blind man is beautiful, and the colors of the intersection perfectly resemble the downtown of a busy city. If he'd had a bit more time, the finished painting could have turned out really well.

Jorge isn't the only person who didn't finish. Of the fifteen, only nine of us have a finished work. Two girls console each other while a third stands by her easel with tears in her eyes. The other two, whoever they are, have already left the room.

Lish tells Jorge she likes his painting like it is, only half-finished. He blushes when she asks if he'll sell it to her. He promises to give it to her as a present once the competition is over.

She doesn't pretend to like mine.

"It's as boring as your outfit," she says. I know she's right, but it still annoys me to hear her say it.

"The technique is good," Jorge says, trying to appease me. I don't know why. He should be furious with me right now. My painting's finished, after all. There's no way he'll be picked for the final round with an incomplete piece.

"I guess." Lish shrugs, turning away from me. I'm not used to arguing with Lish. In fact, I don't think in the two years I've known her we've ever fought about anything more intense than what movie we should watch.

I get why she's mad. Lish met me after I'd been rejected from Burke, and she knows how much I've changed since I attended Burke. When I decided to dye my hair blue, Lish came with me and got hers done in pink. Plus, most of the clothes in my closet were bought on her recommendation. She knows me better than anyone.

But she also knows how much I loved this school. She's heard me talk about it for hours on end. She should understand why I am willing to do whatever it takes.

"I think I'll go for a walk," Jorge says, eyeing us both. "Wanna come with me? The judges will probably take a while to decide."

"You go ahead," I say, glancing around the room. "This time I think I'm going to stay put." Ms. Camford is making the rounds, and I want to be at my easel when she arrives.

"I'll come with you," Lish says to Jorge. From the way he grins, I think Jorge is thrilled.

I watch them leave, and then I start studying the other paintings in the room. I only have to be in the top five to make it to the final round. Out of the nine completed ones, I see at least two paintings I know are not as good as mine. One is sloppy, the other just confusing. But there are a few I know are definitely better than mine. Those ones make me nervous.

"Much better than your last piece, Sydney," a voice says from behind me. It's the same voice I heard this morning, only now the tone is soft and warm, like it used to be. I turn around to once again face Miranda. This time she meets my eye and gives me a bright smile. "If I didn't want the scholarship for myself, I'd root for you."

"You know who I am now?" I ask, my voice pinched with sarcasm. Just because I've changed my clothes and covered my hair doesn't mean I'm suddenly an entirely different person.

Miranda lets out a tiny fake laugh. "I knew who you were the moment I saw you this morning. But it doesn't do to associate with, well, outsiders."

Her words burn. They're awfully similar to the ones she said to me two years ago, after I'd been kicked out of Burke. After she'd decided we could no longer be friends.

"So what's changed?" I ask. Not that I care. Miranda looks me over and then eyes my painting.

"You, apparently," she says, and then she steps lightly away, heading back to her easel.

I'm furious. I was crushed when Miranda suddenly turned from a sweet friend to a cruel snob. If she thinks I'll want to be her friend again on the off chance I get back into Burke, she's wrong. Even if I win this scholarship, the past won't be erased. The last two years will still have happened, and I'll still be a changed person.

Or will I?

I face my painting and can now see clearly the bland, emotionless scene I created. This isn't how I paint. This isn't how I want to paint.

This isn't me.

The tap of Ms. Camford's heels grows close. I don't look at her when she nears me. I just stare at my work until she steps up to my right.

"The judges have made their decisions," she says, her voice calm and pleasant, as if she's talking to a stranger. Was my pain so insignificant she doesn't even remember causing it? She reaches forward and places a blue ribbon on my easel. "Congratulations, Miss Hart."

I don't respond. I wait until the headmistress has moved on, and then I slowly turn around to see who else has a blue ribbon. One boy's painting is of a woman sitting on a porch swing with the ghost of a man next to her. Another boy has done a dog with his head hanging out a car window, staring down a long desert highway. There's a girl's lovely image of a pair of broken glasses sitting on top of an open book. And, of course, there's Miranda's painting, a companion piece. This one depicts a sea turtle swimming through a coral reef. The whole scene's been painted from a side view, capturing both the gray sky over the water and the vibrant landscape beneath it.

Miranda sees me studying her painting. She gives me another of her warm smiles, the kind of smiles we used to share across classrooms in this very school.

The expression doesn't warm me. I don't smile back.

Because this isn't me.

I still want to win the scholarship. I want to study at this academy. But if I do, will it mean falling back into the person I used to be? I loved my time at this school. But I love who I am now. And who I am couldn't have existed if I hadn't been evicted from the academy in the first place.

I pack up my things and stow them in the studio for the next day. I have a lot to think about before round three of the brush off begins.

Twelve

I don't go home. After retrieving my backpack from Lish and getting a cold goodbye as she boards the bus, I walk a block or so away from the academy and call my house to tell my mother I won't be home for dinner.

"Sydney, you've been MIA all day. What's so important you can't even tell us where you are?" she scolds. I can hear Ethan asking for juice in the background. Charlie says something I can't understand, and Ethan laughs. I smile.

"Mom, I've been...at Burke," I say slowly. Mom is silent for a minute, and then she clears her throat.

"You've been at Burke," she repeats, her voice skeptical. I let out a long breath, then tell her about the competition. I'd avoided mentioning it so far. Mom would have been mortified to know I was hanging out at Burke looking like I usually do. Mom's mortified when I go to the corner store looking like I usually do. But now I'm in the final round. I guess she deserves to know.

I sit on the sidewalk and tell her all about the brush off. By the time I explain about being in the final, Mom is so happy I think she might actually start crying.

"Oh, Sydney, this is just what we need," she says, and I hate the way she says *we*, as if both of us were kicked out of the academy.

"Yeah, I know. It's great," I say, trying to match her enthusiasm. It is great, and I should be more excited than Mom is about tomorrow.

"Well, whenever you get home, I'll cook you something for dinner. An omelet maybe?" It's the first time I think my mother's ever offered to cook me something fresh after I've been late for a meal. Omelets are my favorite, but just the thought of eating right now makes my stomach curdle.

"Sounds good," I say before I wrap up the call.

I dig through my pack until I find the cracked mirror shoved in the bottom. Breaking a mirror is supposed to be bad luck, but the day I broke this one was the day I did my first performance on the boardwalk. It was a great performance, and a great day. Since then I've kept the mirror nearby as a reminder that luck is not something that happens—it's something you make for yourself.

I use it now to study my reflection. Only a few hours ago I was thrilled by my simple appearance. Now I just look drab and ugly. On someone like Miranda, this outfit would be nice. On me, it just looks stupid.

But I know it's what I have to do. Isn't getting back into Burke worth a style change?

I put the mirror away and stand up. I don't know why I decided not to go home tonight. The competition is over for the day, and people will be clearing out of the academy soon so they can close up for the night.

I walk back toward the school anyway. When the stone walls come into view, I veer off the path leading to the main entrance and instead, head around the side of the building. I shouldn't be doing this, but I don't even hesitate. I count the first-floor windows as I walk along the gray-stoned wall until I reach the fifth one. I peer inside and see a dark, empty room.

I tap on the glass with my fist, and after a few hits the loose lock unlatches. I slide the window up and slip inside.

This dance studio is small. There are several rooms for dance instruction at the academy, as well as a massive studio on the third floor, directly above the art room I was painting in today. The room I stand in now is used for private instruction or group practice. Since it's summer, the room is empty, but during the school year, spare shoes, towels and notebooks can usually be found stacked on the floor or hung over the barre.

The dancers at Burke have always snuck into this room after school hours. Some of the older girls used it as a way to get in and out of the school on nights when they wanted to go to parties in the city. For the younger dancers, like me and Miranda and others in our year, the space was used for extra practice or to escape the clamor of the dorms when we needed peace and quiet.

I need peace and quiet now. I sit on the floor, staring at myself in the mirror. I kick off my shoes and pull my legs in so I'm sitting cross-legged. Then I change my mind and stand. I get out my phone and scroll through my music playlist.

I pick one of the only classical pieces I still have uploaded, and I plug in my earbuds.

Music flows softly through my head. I spend a moment catching the rhythm of the song. Then I dance.

I stretch my leg up and spin in a slow circle. I try to remember what my instructors would have said to me if I were dancing now as a Burke student. *Chin up! Hip out! Balance!* I drop my leg and raise myself onto my toes. I patter across the room, and do several fouetté turns. My right foot wobbles, and I almost topple over. *Not good enough, Miss Hart! Check your position!* I leap as well as I can in my tight black jeans. Then I stand perfectly still, trying to mimic the grace of a true dancer. Already I can feel the tension in my shoulders, my spine, my hamstrings.

The tempo of the song picks up, and the gentle melody becomes a fast, spirited tune. I love fast music. The more chaotic, the better. I don't need to catch the beat when it changes. A smile spreads across my lips, and I continue my dance, picking up speed along with the instruments on the track. I forget about the instructors of my past. I forget about my posture and my poise. My movements become looser, more relaxed. I spin and step my way across the darkened room. I twirl again and bend in a contraction, stretching my arms forward and taking several steps backward before I straighten my spine once more.

My bandanna begins to slip, and I pull it off with a flourish, throwing it over the barre. I unleash my hair, dropping the braid down my back and then taking out the elastic so the strands come loose. I laugh, relieved to see the vibrant blue again in my reflection, as if I'd secretly been afraid it had disappeared under the cover of the bandanna.

I've never painted to classical music before. But I can imagine what it would be like to paint right now. I jump, throwing my head back and curling my legs behind me so my hair brushes my toes. I land and make a quick pirouette. As the music crashes into a loud finale, I pretend I'm finishing off a brand-new painting. I shake my hair and do a couple of jazz steps, followed by a barrel jump, my body twisting in midair and landing in a low crouch.

A movement in the mirror makes me pause. I stiffen, straightening my back and pulling out my earbuds. I spin around to see Miranda standing by the door.

Thirteen

"**Y**our form is terrible," Miranda says coolly from the doorway. She stands with her arms across her chest, her foot tapping impatiently against the floor.

I can't believe I didn't notice her standing there. I want to curl up in a ball until she goes away.

"I didn't think anyone would be around," I say. I grab my bandanna from the barre and put my shoes on again.

"This is a classroom for Burke students, you know," Miranda replies, stepping into the room. "It's considered breaking and entering when you don't go here."

"It's breaking and entering even if you do go here," I correct her. I may be embarrassed by her having seen my dance, but I'm not going to let her intimidate me. "I was just letting off steam. I'll leave."

"If you won the scholarship, you'd be expected to take art, not dance," she says as I turn toward the window. I stop and look back over my shoulder.

"I know. I want to take art. But that doesn't mean I can't take dance as well," I say.

Miranda presses her lips into a thin line. She looks like she's trying to decide what to say next. "You were never much of a dancer," she says at last.

I twist around to face her again, trying not to let her words hurt as much as they do. "Why would you say something like that, Miranda?" I ask, hoping my voice sounds strong. "I'm no threat to you."

Something flashes across Miranda's eyes. I can see it, even in the darkness of the room. But then she smiles. "No, you're not. You never were either. That's why I kept you around."

"What?" I stare at her, stunned. As horrible as Miranda was after I left the academy, I never doubted our friendship during our years here together.

Miranda takes another step toward me. "You were never any good as a dancer. And you always made me look better by comparison." My eyes sting with tears, but I blink them away. "You have real promise as a painter though," she adds, although her eyes are laughing. "So long as you can keep from dancing around like a lunatic. The Burke Academy has a reputation to uphold, after all. We can't have nonsense like that around here."

I'm surprised Miranda seems to know about my dancing while I paint, but I don't question it. Instead, I find myself defending my artistic style.

"Performance painting is a highly respected form of artistry," I say, my voice calm, almost friendly. I refuse to let Miranda rile me up. "Some of the biggest art galleries in the world have showcased it. And maybe I wasn't a good dancer, but dancing helps make me a better painter. For me, painting works better as an act performed in front of people. It's like an extension of dance and music."

I don't realize how wide I'm grinning until I catch my reflection in the wall-to-wall mirror. I love talking about art. I love talking about performance art. I'm proud to call myself a performance artist.

I study myself smiling into the mirror, and then I see Miranda scowling behind me. She turns and heads for the door.

"Do whatever you like in the final tomorrow," she mutters, her feet practically stomping against the floor. "I can't wait to watch you fail." She storms out of the room, slamming the door behind her. I stare at the place where she was standing and slowly start to understand her short temper and her faltering moods.

Miranda was my friend because she was better than I was at dancing. But when I joined the brush off, she was mean. Only after I changed my outfit and painted in a different, safer way did she start being nice to me again. Which means she must have considered me a threat—until she saw my second painting. And now that she's seen me dancing, I might be a threat again.

I sit back on the floor and dial Lish's number on my phone.

"I've discovered something," I say as soon as she answers.

"The meaning of life?" Lish teases.

I'm glad she's not still mad. "Maybe the meaning of my life," I say.

She sounds curious now. "Okay, so what did you discover?"

I take a deep breath. "That I liked my life when I attended Burke. But I like my life now too." I twist hair around the fingers of my free hand. The blue strands are soft and bright and beautiful.

"So?" Lish is impatient. Lish is always impatient. It's one of the things I love about her. "What did you decide?"

"I don't know." I sigh. "The academy would still be a great place to go, and this time it would be different. I would be a painter. Lish, I could learn so much! But…" I pause, and unravel the hair from my fingers. "I still have some things to figure out. Starting with you."

"With me?" Lish asks, confused.

"If I did get into Burke again, would you stop being my friend?" I have to ask. I remember how hard it was losing Miranda as a friend, and Lish is a better friend than Miranda ever was. I don't want to go through that again. I don't want to lose two best friends over something as stupid as where I go to school.

"You mean if you ditch me?" Lish says, her voice full of the snark she uses when we're having fun together. I am relieved to hear her playful tone. "No, I won't stop being your friend," she continues. "You can't get rid of me that easily."

I relax my shoulders. "Good."

"Anything else I can help you with this evening?" She says it in a prim voice, like she's some sort of telephone operator.

I laugh. "No. The rest I have to figure out for myself."

"Well, then, I'd better get going. See you tomorrow at the brush off?"

"I still don't know," I admit.

"I'll see you tomorrow," Lish says, and we say our goodbyes before I hang up the phone.

Lish is convinced I'll compete tomorrow, but I'm not so sure. It's funny how quickly things can change. This afternoon I was willing to buy a new outfit just to impress the judges and earn my spot in the final round. Now, I don't think it's worth losing my personality just to attend a good school. I paint with music, and movement, and mess. What's the point of having good teachers if I have to give up the things that make me love art?

Unless, of course, I don't have to give them up.

I started the brush off as myself, and I made it through the first round. It could have been luck. But it could have been something else too. It could have meant the judges liked what they saw.

If I compete tomorrow as the girl I used to be, I'll be stepping back into my old life.

But what if I compete as the girl I am now? Is it worth the gamble, to show them what I'm really capable of?

Fourteen

The final round is scheduled to begin at 2:00 PM on Sunday afternoon. I'm up by seven. I tossed and turned all night, dreaming I showed up late.

I spend a long time choosing what to wear. Normally I don't care much about my clothes, but for this occasion I think the right look is crucial. I channel my inner Lish and try on at least six different outfits before I find a winning combination. Then I sneak into Mom's room and start going through her closet.

"Whatcha doing?"

I jump, startled by the squeaky voice of my brother.

"I'm looking for a coat," I say, and then I kneel down next to Ethan. "Don't tell Mom, okay?"

Mom wouldn't appreciate me going through her things without her permission, but she would never let me borrow the coat I'm after even if I asked. I'll return it before she ever notices it's gone. No harm, no foul.

Ethan considers me for a moment, his head tilted to one side. He looks like a puppy dog, with his big brown eyes and unruly bed head.

"Okay," he says at last, and I give him a hug before sending him downstairs for breakfast.

It takes me less than a minute to locate the coat shoved into the back of Mom's closet. It's long and heavy, meant for colder weather than a muggy July day like this one promises to be. Mom used to wear this coat everywhere in the winter, until she lost her job at the marketing firm and fell out of touch with the rich executives she once spent all her time with. Now Mom works for the Nova Scotia tourism board. The job's okay, but she misses the way things were before. She never wears this coat anymore, but I know she'd love to.

I stay in my glow-in-the-dark lightning-bolt pajamas when I go down for breakfast. The entire family is there, Ethan eating a bowl of cereal, and Mom and Charlie drinking coffee as they talk about what housework they want to get done this morning.

Mom smiles when she sees me. It's not the typical response I get when I walk around the house in my pajamas. Normally she grumbles about it being tacky not to dress first before coming downstairs. But today she gives me a happy glance when I shuffle into the kitchen. She doesn't even complain when I pour myself a cup of coffee.

"We thought we would come and watch you today, Sydney," Mom says while I'm loading my coffee with milk and sugar. My shoulders tense, and I almost spill milk all over the counter.

"You what?" I ask, twirling around to face the table.

Mom's eyes shine with a liveliness I haven't seen in a long time. "We thought it would be fun to watch you paint this afternoon."

I stare at her, dumbfounded. I wasn't expecting an audience today. Well, okay, I was, but not an audience made up of my family. I want to tell her she's not allowed to come. I want to tell her I don't want her to come. I want to put my hand in the air and simply shout, "NO!"

But I can't. She looks so excited. Mom never looks excited anymore.

"That's...g-great, Mom," I stutter, forcing a smile and then quickly turning back to the counter. "Thanks."

The coffee is hot, but I gulp it down anyway. The heat keeps me occupied. It stops me from thinking about how disastrous today might be with my mother watching. When the cup is half empty, I grab a protein bar from the cupboard and try to escape back to my room.

"Where are you going?" Ethan asks when I'm two steps away from being free of the family.

"I'm going to...prepare," I say, giving everyone another fake grin. "For later."

"You should eat something heartier," Charlie says, eyeing my peanut-butter oat bar with distaste. "Keep your strength up. It's an important day. You don't want to load up on too much sugar or too many carbs."

Charlie's an amateur health nut. He's one of those annoying people who likes to tell you how bad everything you're eating is before he scarfs down a bag of chips and follows it up with a king-size energy drink.

"I'll eat something good for lunch," I promise. He's right about needing to keep my strength up, but I also don't want to eat so much I get nervous and vomit at the brush off.

"Let us know when you're ready to go, and we'll drive over together," Mom says. I look down at the coffee mug in my left hand. It's yellow, with painted bumblebees buzzing around a golden beehive.

"Oh, I, um, I told Lish we'd take the bus," I lie. I can't do anything about having Mom at the competition. She'll see me paint, and she'll know I borrowed her designer coat. But I can stop her from giving me presentation tips the entire ride over to the academy.

"Okay. Well, we can meet you there then, I guess." Mom sounds disappointed, but I only nod and rush out of the kitchen before she can say anything else.

I don't want to hurt her feelings. And I'm glad she's excited about today. I just wish she was excited about my painting, not about the chance for me to get back into the academy. I don't want her to be annoyed if I lose. I want her to be impressed by my effort, not angry at the result.

She hasn't seen me paint in a while. I don't think she has a clue what to expect. If she did, she probably wouldn't be planning a family outing to come watch.

Fifteen

slip out of the house at eleven and ride the bus by myself. It takes an hour to reach the stop closest to the Burke Academy. When I arrive, Lish is already waiting for me. We go to a nearby bistro for lunch, and I heed Charlie's warning about eating a good meal. With the little I have left over from yesterday's shopping, I order a salad, breadsticks and a glass of lemonade. I wear Mom's coat, the flats I bought yesterday and my black bandanna over my hair the entire time. It's incredibly hot under all the dark fabrics, and the lemonade helps keep me cool.

We get to the school a little after one o'clock. Inside the nice cool foyer, there are signs directing visitors to the auditorium, where the final round will be held. I don't need directions. I've danced on the auditorium stage dozens of times.

The inside of the auditorium looks exactly like a small theater, with curved rows of chairs and tracks of dim lights lining the aisles. I'm surprised to see a camera crew near the front row, and two portable screens set up on either side of the stage. It takes me a moment to understand they're for the competition, so people sitting near the back can still see what is on each painter's canvas.

"Quite the production, eh?"

I turn around to see Jorge standing with his hands in the pockets of his jeans. He watches two teenage volunteers adjusting the height of one of the screens.

"What are you doing here?" I ask. I figured Jorge would be at home today, since he didn't advance after the second round.

"I wanted to see how you do," he says, as if I should have already guessed his reason for coming. He doesn't seem upset about not still being in the competition. In fact, he looks happy about getting to watch the final round as a member of the audience.

I stare at him, confused. "Why did you tell me about the brush off?" I finally ask.

Jorge crinkles his eyebrows, looking as puzzled as I am.

"I thought you should compete," he says. He tries to make it sound casual, but there's a tightness to his words. I keep staring at him, and Lish does too. After an awkward pause, he pulls his hands from his pockets and crosses his arms over his chest. "See, I'm in the year below you. Or I *was*, when you went here. We never met, but I remember what happened. The whole academy knew about your dismissal, and I thought it was horrible of them to make you leave just because your mom got laid off. Anyway, at the beginning of the summer I was on the boardwalk, and I recognized the name on your sign."

I smile. *Art by hArt.* Lish is the one who insisted I have a sign up whenever I perform. I never really saw the value of it, but I guess the sign was worthwhile after all.

"I watched some of your performances, and I thought you were good. So when the competition came around, I figured I should let you know."

"Wow. Thanks, Jorge," I say with surprise.

He shakes his head and then looks to his right. "Don't thank me," he says. "I didn't really do anything. And I hate to be the bearer of bad news, but I think you've got your work cut out for you today."

I follow his gaze to a display of the finalists' paintings from the first two rounds. I saw them all yesterday, but hadn't paid much attention to them beyond how they compared to my work. Now I walk over to the display and carefully study each piece.

I see what Jorge means. The other paintings are good. Really good. How had I not noticed? The picture of the woman sitting next to the ghost has great lines and a remarkable use of shadow. The dog looking out at the highway has so much yearning in his eyes, I can almost hear him howling. One of the first-round pieces, from the life theme, is of a little girl walking in the rain, her face lit up at the sight of someone waiting for her in the distance. Happiness radiates from the oils on the canvas, and after staring at the sogginess of the girl's surroundings, a cold shiver actually runs down my spine.

I look at my paintings last. The second piece I did—the bird flying over the land—is just as bland today as it was yesterday. My first picture of the dead forest has a few obvious mistakes, but I like it more. It suits me better. It's got more depth.

But neither painting reaches the level of my competitors'. The other works on display have been done by people who have had years of practice, working with great teachers. Which is why I'm here in the first place, isn't it? To get a chance to study at the same level as these painters. Even if the four other finalists aren't already students of the academy, they've clearly been practicing their art for a long time.

I want to learn how to paint like these people. But if I'm going to compete one more time, I have to take the risk and try to win as the person I am, not as the person I think the academy wants me to be.

Sixteen

B y the time the third round begins, the auditorium is more than half full. I would never
have guessed there'd be this many people
interested in watching five teenagers speed-paint.
It took a while before I could even locate my
family sitting near the back doors. I'm still not
thrilled Mom will be watching this final round,
but I'm glad Ethan is here to cheer me on.

I sit in the front with the other finalists while
Ms. Camford thanks everyone for attending
and explains how the brush off's final round
will happen. This time the setup is different. We
will go onstage one at a time, with our backs to
the audience so everyone can watch us as we
paint. Each of us will have a different theme,

so one person doesn't have longer to prepare than anyone else.

Our order of appearance was decided on a first-come, first-served basis. I made sure I signed up last. Miranda is going first.

The lights dim, and Miranda makes her way backstage. I peer around at the other people in the front row, trying to figure out who the judges are. Just as in the first two rounds, no one carries a clipboard or a pin labeling them as a judge. I study everyone until the lights go out and a single spotlight brightens the stage.

Miranda walks out and stands by her canvas, her hands clasped in front of her. She's wearing a white cardigan and a beige skirt. My guess is, she wants to show the judges she can paint a whole picture without making any mess.

"Miranda Wakefield," Ms. Camford announces, "your theme for today is 'heritage.' You have five minutes. Your time starts now."

Miranda doesn't waste a single second. She picks up a brush and begins to paint as if she knows exactly what she's going to do. Maybe she does. The screens on either side of the stage show zoomed-in versions of her canvas as she makes quick, feathery strokes with her brush. She only uses a couple of colors, shades of cream and brown, giving the whole picture the look of an old photograph. As the image takes form, I understand why she chose the colors she did. The painting she is creating is of a girl in a modern sundress looking at a framed picture of another girl with practically the same face—a great-grandmother, maybe—wearing an outfit from the early 1900s.

"One minute," Ms. Camford warns, but Miranda doesn't need to worry. Her picture is finished with forty or so seconds to spare. She uses the remaining time to add wisps of hair around the modern girl's ears, and in her final ten seconds, she quickly gives the girl's sundress some polka dots. When Ms. Camford says her time is up, Miranda daintily places her brush back down and steps away from her canvas. She gives a small bow and then walks confidently offstage.

"She's good," the girl beside me says. She's right. Miranda used her five minutes perfectly. The painting of the girl looking at the photo from her past fits her theme well. Plus, it's a good painting. It doesn't look like it was done in only five minutes. I'm not surprised, but I am nervous. I don't know how anyone will top what she's done.

Next up is one of the boys, and his theme is "wilderness." He pauses for a full thirty seconds before he approaches his canvas. When he starts painting, he quickly makes a wintry forest full of animals bounding around and playing in the snow. It's a nice painting, but I can tell he's not happy with it. He probably spent those first thirty seconds trying, and failing, to come up with a unique idea for the theme. His smile is tight when he takes his bow, and he stalks off the stage with the air of someone about to throw a tantrum once he's out of sight.

I don't see the other two performances. When the next boy is getting ready to go up, I slip out of my seat and exit the auditorium. Jorge is waiting for me in the hallway, right where I asked him to be.

"Did you get it all set up?" I ask.

He grins, nodding his head. "It's all ready," he says. "I'm so glad you're doing this."

I smile. "I am too. Thanks for helping me, Jorge."

"No problem. You'd better get ready. You'll be up in no time!" Jorge pushes me toward the backstage entrance before he heads up to the technical booth over the stage.

I double-checked the competition rules. We're allowed to use our own props for painting, as long as we don't have anything that makes the actual painting process faster. So I've asked Jorge to go up to the booth and plug in my phone for a bit of mood music.

I spend a minute by myself, and then I go backstage. Miranda and both of the boys are waiting there, watching the fourth painter from the wings. I hear applause, and soon the girl who had been sitting beside me hurries to join us backstage. She looks pleased with her work. I give her a thumbs-up as she passes by me, and she smiles in return.

The volunteers clear away the girl's easel and set up mine in its place. Then one of the volunteers tells me to head out onstage.

As I walk past Miranda, she eyes my long coat skeptically.

"Good luck," she says. Her voice is cold again. It's supposed to intimidate me, but instead it has the opposite effect. If Miranda was sure I would fail, she'd give me an encouraging smile.

Her cruel words only suggest she's still afraid I might pull off something spectacular.

I ignore her mean expression and step out onto the spotlit stage.

Seventeen

Being on this stage makes me feel like I'm about to start one of my old recitals. Only I was never a good-enough dancer to perform as a soloist. I'm not sure I'm a strong-enough painter to be up here now either. At least, I'm not strong enough yet. I know I have a ways to go before I can match the skills of the other competitors now watching me from backstage. So if I want a shot at getting the scholarship, I have to do something special.

Which is exactly what I have planned.

I can barely see Ms. Camford when she stands from her front-row seat, but I hear her words clearly as they carry through her microphone.

"Sydney Hart," she says, and my breath catches in my throat when I hear her saying my name. I flash back to when she told me I could no longer attend the Burke Arts Academy. I've never known if she was sorry to see me leave, but it doesn't matter now. The only important thing now is what I'm about to accomplish.

I stand up straight, my black coat flowing down to my feet.

"Your theme for today is..."

I press my lips together, waiting for the reveal.

"'You.'"

I want to be surprised at the theme. I want to gawk at the idea of having to use myself as a painting subject. But I don't have time. Without missing a beat, Ms. Camford continues. "You have five minutes. Your time starts now."

I stand still for one second, two, three. Then I nod, signaling to Jorge to press *Play* on my phone.

When the beat starts, I smile. I glimpse the confused looks of the people in the front row, but I don't waste time trying to gauge their reactions. With the first chords of my favorite Wayward Tides song blaring down over the auditorium, I slip off the black flats. I slide off the black coat. I pull away the black bandanna.

And then it's just me standing there. Me, in my torn, flower-printed leggings. Me, in my green T-shirt with the bright-purple smiley face. Me, with long blue hair falling past my shoulders.

I rise up onto my toes and lift one leg high in the air. I grab a brush and dip it in some paint. I switched back to acrylics this time, the same set I use whenever I'm working outdoors. I smear the paint onto the bristles of the brush, and then I begin.

And soon it becomes just another performance on the boardwalk, with the Halifax Harbour behind me and the sun beaming down from a bright, hot sky. I slash the canvas with streaks of brown before I've even decided what I'm going to paint. It looks like a floor. So a floor is what it becomes. I think about myself, who I am, why I'm here. I take a few seconds to bend and do a back walkover, raising first one and then the other leg in a graceful, slow flip. Then I grab a new brush and scribble a furious wall of beige. I've created a room, and suddenly I know what I want the room to represent.

I add a dark line across the wall, and a silver rectangle of a mirror. It's a dance studio, like the ones here at the academy. Like the one I danced in only yesterday.

I work on myself next. I draw the outline of a girl with a straight back and a tight bun of brown hair. She stands facing away from the wall with the mirror. She looks out of a window. She looks lost, unsure.

I mix colors on my palette while I tap my feet along to the music. Then I throw my head back, my hair billowing out behind me, as I start creating the window. It's difficult, but I do my best to give the impression of glass. I make the window stretch across the canvas, so the dance studio can be seen through it. But when I get to where the girl stands—where I stand—I make the glass shatter outward.

I do a series of four fast pirouettes. Then I hold my right leg out to the side as I paint one broken piece of glass in which the lost girl's face is reflected. In the glass, she has blue hair, and she smiles. She's confident, and she's happy.

"One minute remaining," Ms. Camford says, her voice strained through the microphone as she works to be heard over the pounding music.

I finish the girl's reflection, and I put a few more strokes of paint on the shattering bits of glass so they look like they're flying through the air. Then I take a deep breath and prepare for the finale I can't resist attempting.

With one hand I pick up my canvas and toss it across the stage. It skids over the black wood and comes to a stop several feet away. I drop my paintbrush and loop my hair into a quick bun so it doesn't get in my way. Then I start the best part of any performance. I dip my fingers into different colors of paint, and in a rush of movement I step toward my painting. My paint-covered fingers press onto the canvas as I cartwheel over it.

I twist, crouch and then somersault back toward my easel, grabbing the painting on the way. When I stand, I hold the painting with one hand and use my free fingers to smudge the fingerprints of paint, adding glints of color to the tinkling glass shards.

The painting is done. I have just enough time left to add my signature.

Normally I kiss the picture, signing it with a thick coat of lipstick. But today I need to step it up. They might think I'm overdoing things for shock value. Maybe I am. But I have no choice. I have to go all out.

I smear my hand into the glob of bright-red paint I've so far left untouched on my palette. I wipe my palm across my mouth, covering my lips and a good portion of my face with paint. I let the audience see what I'm doing. Then I grin and bend in and kiss the bottom corner of the painting.

I wipe some of the paint off my face with my arm. I start to bow, then change my mind and do a handstand instead. I stay on my hands until Ms. Camford tells me my time is up.

I drop my legs and stand upright next to my painting. Jorge has faded out the music, and for a long moment there is nothing but silence in the auditorium. Then the applause begins.

It's thunderous. And it's the best sound I've ever heard.

Eighteen

"You are crazy!" Lish says. She meets me outside the stage area, a huge grin on her face. "You are so crazy!" She throws her arms around me, and I laugh, tightly hugging her back.

"I know. They probably hated it," I say. It might be true. They really may have hated what I did. But I'm not worried about it. I feel good right now. I feel like I've just accomplished something amazing.

"Anyone who hated that doesn't know anything about a good show," Lish assures me.

"Well, I must have no clue what makes a good show then," Miranda says. I didn't see her backstage when I finished. The other painters offered me stunned congratulations, but Miranda was nowhere in sight.

She's here now, however. And she's looking at me like I'm a bug she wants to squish under her foot.

"You, clueless? Yeah, sounds about right," Lish says. I haven't introduced Lish to Miranda, but she's obviously put the name together with my stories. Now she stares Miranda down while Miranda tries to ignore her by scowling at me instead.

"You look ridiculous, you know," she says, her hands pressed to her hips, "with paint all over your face. Are you, like, six?"

Her cruelty still hurts. I remember when we were friends, and I wish we could still be friends now. But I also remember what she said yesterday. Whether she ever liked me or not, Miranda only became my friend when I made her look like a better dancer. She has her good qualities. She's a good student, a great dancer and a talented artist too. But being a true friend is not one of Miranda's strengths. I have to accept her for who she is, even if it means we'll never get along again.

I fix my eyes on her and smile as sincerely as I can.

"Thanks for your support, Miranda," I say, like I'm completely serious. "It really means a lot." Before she can stop me, I step toward her and give her a hug. She's too surprised to struggle against me. I squeeze her tightly, the same way I squeezed Lish a moment ago. Then I pull back and plant a kiss on her cheek. A red lip mark stains her pale skin, and Miranda starts to tremble with rage. She opens her mouth to respond, but before she can, Lish grabs my arm and pulls me away.

"Come on," she says, her voice barely containing her glee, "let's get you cleaned up. You're awesome, but you do look funny with paint all over your face."

I go to the nearest bathroom to wash off the paint. Then Lish and I meet Jorge by the auditorium's entrance.

"Thanks again for your help," I tell him as he hands back my phone.

"Yeah, good job, boy," Lish says.

"It's Jorge. J-O-R-G-E!" Jorge exclaims.

Lish nods. "B-O-Y. Got it." She brushes past Jorge and heads back into the auditorium.

The winner of the brush off will be announced in about ten minutes. Jorge watches her go, then turns back to me.

"You know, Lish has a terrific memory," I tell him. He gives me a confused look, and I smile. "She remembers everyone's name as soon as she hears it. She only messes up the names of people she likes."

"Oh." Jorge blushes. Then a small smile creeps onto his lips, and he follows Lish into the auditorium.

I watch him go, but I don't follow him inside. Not yet. The winner will be announced soon, but I want to take a couple of minutes to be proud of what I did before I find out who will be receiving the scholarship. I might not win. In fact, I probably won't. But as much as I want to attend Burke again, even if I lose I have to be glad I tried. It will be hard, with Mom complaining and Miranda gloating and everyone else feeling sorry for me. So I take the time to be glad now. I feel the looseness of my limbs, and the breathlessness after my performance. I feel the smile spreading wide across my face. I let myself be happy, and then, only then, I enter the auditorium.

Now is the time to hope for the best.

Nineteen

Ms. Camford stands in the middle of the stage, the five final paintings lined up in a row to her right. My painting is less polished than the others. Next to Miranda's photograph girl and the one boy's forest are a rotating planet and a landscape of Niagara Falls. I'm curious to know what the other themes were. All four of the pictures are good, but I'm proud of my painting too. Even if it is a bit more wild than the others.

"The Burke Arts Academy's first ever brush-off competition for young painters has been a marvelous success," Ms. Camford says. She smiles warmly out at the audience, and there's a short round of applause before she continues. "Outstanding talent was showcased here today, and the decision to name one painter as the winner has been extremely difficult. All five painters this afternoon have shown enthusiasm, adaptability and originality in their work. They should all be proud of their accomplishments today." There's more clapping.

I sit with the other painters, wishing she'd just get on with it. My impressionist painting sticks out like a sore thumb next to everyone else's more traditional achievements. I won't be surprised to see the scholarship go to someone else. Still, the waiting is horrible.

"I'm happy now to invite our special guest judge out onstage to announce the winner," Ms. Camford says. "The Galbraith family has been gracious enough to sponsor one young artist to attend the Burke Arts Academy, and it is a joy to now introduce to you a member of that family, Mrs. Genevieve Galbraith."

A woman with long, sleek black hair walks out onto the stage. The spotlight catches the stud in her nose. It glints with light, and as I see it shine, I suddenly realize why the name Galbraith sounded so familiar. I know Genevieve Galbraith. She's a local artist. I saw one of her exhibitions last winter at the Art Gallery of Nova Scotia here in Halifax. Her work is incredible. I can't believe she's the one sponsoring the scholarship.

"Thank you," Genevieve says as she takes the microphone, her voice deep and melodic, with an Acadian accent. She flips her hair back behind her shoulder. "When I was a girl, I attended the Burke Arts Academy. I loved this school, its teachers and my fellow students. But academically, I always struggled. Whether it was in core subjects, like science or math, or performance classes in dance or music, I could never reach the level of my friends. Because of that, I often felt left out, like I didn't belong. But then, in my fourth year at the Burke Academy, I took a visual art class. And it changed my life."

I lean forward in my seat. I'd had no idea Genevieve Galbraith was a Burke student.

"Learning to paint, draw and sculpt set me free," Genevieve continues. "It gave me the chance to express myself in a way I'd never been able to do before. So when my family and I decided to sponsor a student here at the academy, I wanted to find someone who showed, above everything else, a passion for art and the potential to benefit from the education few institutions can provide like the Burke Arts Academy can. Which is why I'm happy to announce the result of today's wonderful competition."

She pulls a small envelope from the pocket of her shimmering silver cardigan. She opens the envelope and draws out a slip of paper. It's like a Hollywood awards ceremony. I try to breathe normally, but my heart is thumping uncomfortably in my chest. "The winner of the first ever Burke Arts Academy brush-off competition is..."

I hold my breath. Genevieve smiles out at the audience and then scans the first row until she finds the five painters. She looks at all of us. Then she locks eyes with me.

"Sydney Hart."

I let out my breath. I am so dizzy, I think I might pass out.

Twenty

I don't faint.

Thank goodness.

With shaking hands and wobbly legs, I manage to creep up onto the stage and accept my award. I even survive the onslaught of congratulatory hugs from my friends and family afterward. Even Mom can't hide her excitement. I got what I wanted and what she wanted too. I'm back in the academy.

Only this time, I'm here as a painter. And I can't think of anything better.

After the commotion dies down, Genevieve finds me in the academy's lobby. We walk to the school's inner courtyard and sit on a stone bench donated years ago by the family of another Burke graduate.

"I wasn't sure if I should choose you," Genevieve admits. "The Burke Arts Academy is strict. And when you tried so hard to blend in during the second round, I thought you might be too restrained if you attended a place like this. It takes a strong will to be an individual here. I should know."

I'm not upset by her words. I'm glad she was noticing the painters during the brush off. I'm glad she didn't only look at what they put on the canvas.

"So why did you change your mind?" I ask.

Genevieve smiles. "I decided, along with the other judges, to give you a chance in the final. Then I learned from your headmistress that you used to attend the academy. I knew you must have been serious about the competition, if you were willing to face coming here again. And then your final performance, well, it showed me you weren't willing to ignore your true personality either."

"Thank you for giving me a chance," I say. "I won't let you down."

"It will still be tough, but I think you can handle it. I saw your signature on Miss Wakefield's cheek." Her eyes sparkle with amusement.

"Besides, I think you can add something special to this school. I don't know if the Burke Arts Academy has ever had a performer of the visual arts before. I love the concept though. In fact, I've been thinking of teaching my students about it as well."

"You're a teacher?" I ask.

Genevieve shakes her head. "No. Not really. I run workshops at art galleries around Nova Scotia. And I have a workshop coming up in the fall here in Halifax that would be perfect for introducing performing art. Would you be interested in joining me? I would love to give a demonstration."

I blink in surprise. "Really? You want me to perform?"

"If you're interested. I think it could be a lot of fun, and a fantastic learning opportunity for both of us," Genevieve says.

"Yeah, I think so too." I nod. I've never thought about teaching people art before. But I love talking about what I do. Maybe I'd love teaching it too.

We talk for a while longer. I ask Genevieve about her time at Burke and her life as an artist now. She tells me about her schooling and her favorite local artists. She even invites me to her next exhibition at the end of the summer. When we say goodbye, I know it will not be for long. Genevieve will be at the meeting my mother and I have scheduled with Ms. Camford next week, to go over the details of my re-enrollment.

Back inside the school, I meet up with Lish and Jorge.

"So what are you going to do now?" Lish asks, her arm around my shoulder.

"Well, I have to meet with Ms. Camford to collect my cash prize and go over a bit of academy stuff before our meeting," I say. "And then I need to start preparing for art camp in a couple of weeks. But before I do that, how about some food?" I look at Lish, and I grin. "While we eat, I can read through the academy's handbook."

"School doesn't start for another month and a half," Lish says. "Why do you need to read the handbook now?"

"Because..." I laugh. "I need to see what it says about students having blue hair."

MERE JOYCE writes short stories as well as novels and holds a Master of Library and Information Science from the University of Western Ontario. The library where she works is also a public art gallery that often showcases contemporary forms of art. The organization hosts an annual brush-off competition for teens. Mere lives in Cambridge, Ontario, with her family. For more information, visit www.merejoyce.com.